ZOM-B

D1336126

ZOM-B CIRCUS

DARREN SHAN

SIMON AND SCHUSTER

First published in Great Britain in 2014 by Simon & Schuster UK Ltd
A CBS COMPANY

1 3 5 7 9 10 8 6 4 2

Simon & Schuster UK Ltd
1st Floor
222 Gray's Inn Road
London WC1X 8HB

www.simonandschuster.co.uk

Simon & Schuster Australia, Sydney
Simon & Schuster India, New Delhi

A CIP catalogue copy for this book
is available from the British Library.

PB ISBN: 978-1-47112-272-9
EBOOK ISBN: 978-1-47112-273-6

Printed and bound by CPI Group (UK) Ltd, Croydon, CR0 4YY

For:

The real Cat(herine) Ward – more ruthless than this version by far!

Editorial ringmaster:

Elv Moody.

Agenting jugglers:

the Christopher Little clowns.

ONE

'There are no second chances in life.'

That was Cat Ward's motto, and she looked round the classroom with a serious expression as she rolled it out, trying to lock gazes with her students.

'If you don't work hard now, you'll be a failure later,' she continued. 'You have to seize every opportunity that you can. This world punishes the weak and indifferent.'

They didn't care. They never listened. They just yawned and scribbled in their books.

Cat decided to give it one more try. 'The future can

be whatever you make of it. You can carry on being failures, or you can choose to change and make the most of the chances that we're providing you with.'

To her surprise, a hand went up. Cat started to smile, until she realised the hand belonged to Becky Smith. A wretched girl, rude and aggressive, but smarter than a lot of the others. She was the one who had given Cat her nickname — *Ward 6*, which was the psychiatric ward in their local hospital.

'Yes, Becky?' Cat said, forcing a smile.

'What you're saying,' Becky sniffed, 'is that if we work really hard, and seize all the chances that come our way, we can be a big success like you.'

'Well, I wouldn't say I was *that* successful,' Cat chuckled modestly.

'You're saying,' Becky continued with relish, 'that we can work in a dump like this and spend all our days trying to drum mathematical equations into the heads of people who don't give a damn.'

Cat's smile faded.

'You're saying,' Becky went on, 'that we can be a laughing stock, work crazy hours for rubbish pay, and spend our long holidays wondering why we feel so bored and useless.'

'That's enough,' Cat snapped.

'What chances have *you* taken in life?' Becky responded.

'I'm warning you,' Cat snarled.

'What?' Becky grinned. 'Will you send me to the principal's office?'

Cat trembled with frustration. She knew the principal had a soft spot for Becky Smith. If she complained about the girl, she'd probably be assigned extra duties as punishment.

'Forget it,' Cat finally said stiffly. 'I wanted to help, but clearly my help isn't appreciated. Let's carry on with the lesson.'

The rest of the period was horrible, Cat going through the motions, unable to get Becky's taunt out of her head. The worst thing was that Cat *did* feel bored and useless. As a child, she had wanted to be an experimental physicist or nuclear engineer. Instead she had become a droning mentor to a pack of simpletons and thugs.

It wasn't fair. She'd always been in the top two or three in her classes in school. Her speciality was mathematics. She'd grown up thinking the world was hers, that she would do wonderful things in her chosen field, become the twenty-first century's Newton or Einstein.

Then she went to university and realised she was no genius. She was in the top ten or fifteen per cent, but no better than that. Academic fame would never be hers. At best she would become a lab assistant to someone more gifted than her.

Losing interest in her career, Cat's standards slipped. She no longer challenged herself, but merely breezed along, angry and bitter, taking the easy options.

Teaching was by no means a soft job, but it was easier to go down that route than look for a less stable position in the world beyond. Cat knew that she would be able to glide along on autopilot as a teacher. It wasn't what she had dreamt of as a child, but it was safe and secure, so she went for it.

She had been teaching maths to surly teenagers like Becky Smith ever since. It had only been five years, but already it felt like she had served a life sentence. She could feel her hair turning grey. Every day was the same, lecturing lifelessly to her students, making small talk with the teachers in the staffroom, watching soap operas and reality shows on TV when she went home.

As the annoyingly intuitive Becky had guessed, she didn't even make use of the long holidays, just sat around moaning to the few friends that she was still in touch with, dreading the start of the new term, but doing nothing to break the cycle. Her only moments of contentment came when, several times a day, she would sneeringly tell one or more of her charges that there were no second chances in life, that they were blowing their futures.

As class ended and Becky trotted off with her friends, to crow about the points she'd scored over their teacher, Cat had to admit that she was in a low and lonely place.

'Something has to change,' she whispered to herself. 'I can't go on like this. I'm better than other people. I just need to be given a chance to prove it.'

Perhaps some higher force was listening, or maybe it was coincidence, but Cat was to be provided with the chance to prove what she was made of just a few days later, when the zombie apocalypse shook the world to its core and the living dead ran wild through her school.

TWO

Cat was on her lunch break when the zombies came storming through the building. There had been rumours of undead outbreaks in Ireland and other countries prior to this, so it didn't come as a complete surprise. Cat had even been joking about the subject with her sister Jules a few nights earlier, and had said that she didn't think she'd notice a difference if all her students turned into zombies.

Still, like most sensible people, Cat had dismissed the rumours. She hadn't been expecting an invasion and, like the majority of her fellow teachers and their students, she froze when she spotted the monsters streaming through the school.

Cat had been on her way to the staffroom, but had stopped when she'd seen a group of girls hanging out in a chemistry lab. They shouldn't have been there. Cat thought about saying nothing, but a few of them would be in her class after lunch and she was worried that they might sneak in some combustible materials and start a fire — it wouldn't be the first time. So, with a sigh, she went in to chase them out.

It should have been a simple eviction, but the girls only laughed when she told them to leave. 'We're not doing any harm, miss,' they protested.

'Out,' she insisted.

'But why?' they whined. 'It's quiet in here. We can do a bit of extra study.'

Cat spent several minutes arguing with them. She could have threatened to report them to the principal – all of the students apart from Becky Smith were wary of Miss Reed – but that would have been a sign of weakness. She had learnt very quickly that if you were to stand up to these little savages you had to do it by yourself.

The girls had almost given up and were on the point of leaving when the screams rang out and they caught sight of the first wave of zombies.

Cat knew with a single glimpse that these were genuine members of the living dead. They were ripping open throats and skulls, lashing out at anyone within reach. They had long fangs and there were bones sticking out of their fingers and toes. They hunted like predators. Each one of them would scratch or bite a few passers-by, then target an individual and bring the victim down, before cracking open the poor person's skull and digging into their brain.

Cat and the girls watched the slaughter with horror. Cat wasn't surprised to see the students who had been wounded start to turn into zombies themselves. It had always been that way in the movies.

Then a few of the zombies set their sights on the group in the chemistry lab and lumbered through the doorway.

That was when Cat came into her own. Reacting instinctively in line with her motto that there were no second chances in life, she grabbed one of the girls and threw her to the advancing zombies. As the girl screamed with terror, Cat grabbed two of the other spiteful cows and pushed them after the first.

The rest of the girls shrieked and ducked out of the way of their teacher, but Cat didn't care. The zombies had stopped to feast on the three she'd propelled at them, giving her a chance to break free before any others came in.

Dashing to the rear of the lab, which overlooked a small courtyard, Cat smashed the window to pieces with a chair. Then she leapt through and set off for the front of the building.

She never looked back, or called to the terrified, helpless girls in the lab to follow her, or spared a thought for the three she had condemned. This wasn't a time for pausing. It was a time for action. Those who seized their chance might get away. The rest would be lost. And Cat Ward had no time for losers.

THREE

The fugitive teacher only barely made it out of the school. It was sheer chaos, the undead running wild, the living thrashing around in a blind panic. It took a cool head to navigate the mayhem, and that day Miss Ward lived up to her name and was one of the coolest *Cats* in London.

She tossed a few more students to the zombies as she fled, along with one of her fellow teachers who was trying to organise the children and lead a gang of them to safety. These sacrifices served to distract the hunting killers and Cat looked for opportunities at every turn. A couple of times she sent young kids flying into walls when there were no zombies present, hoping to knock them out, so that they would attract any brain munchers who might chance along this way later — better they stop to eat the brains of the dazed students than carry on and catch up with her.

It wasn't much quieter on the streets outside. London was a city caught in the grip of an undead menace. Zombies were running wild everywhere. Cat couldn't understand how they had spread so swiftly, but she didn't stop to try and make sense of it. Picking a direction at random, she took off as fast as she could, sparing not a thought for those who were being butchered all around her.

Cat never noticed the strange, semi-human figure who stepped out of the school to stare after her as she fled. If she had glanced back, she might have spotted him, a man standing in the shadows, like no other she had ever seen, with pustulent, peeling flesh, no fingernails, grey hair and yellow eyes.

But, even if she had clocked her sinister observer, she was already too far away to have heard him when he muttered, 'Interesting . . .' And she definitely wouldn't have noticed when he stepped inside, whistled to one of his colleagues and nodded at him to follow Cat at a distance as she fled.

FOUR

The following weeks and months were horrendous, not just for Cat Ward but the entire world. Zombies had swarmed the planet and wiped out civilisation as it had been known. Pockets of the living still existed in most places, but they were under constant threat, having to hole up at night when the undead came out of hiding and went on the prowl.

That was the only positive, Cat mused to herself one sunny afternoon as she explored the streets and shops of north London, searching for food and supplies. Zombies were sensitive to sunlight. It hurt their eyes and caused them discomfort. If they had been able to roam in the daytime as well as by night, it would have been impossible for survivors like Cat to operate.

As it was, Cat had learnt to get along nicely. The first few days and nights had been the hardest as she had no idea where to go or what to do. Should she stay in the city or head for the country? Make her base in an apartment in a tower block or set up home in a house in suburbia? Team up with other survivors or keep to herself?

She made mistakes in those early stages, but just about everybody did. The difference between her and those who succumbed to the zombies was that she learnt from her errors and corrected them.

One mistake she never made – and it was a mistake that cost lots of people their lives – was to put the welfare of anybody else before her own. Cat faced countless zombie attacks over the first couple of weeks. Each time she grabbed the nearest human and threw them to the undead lions, creating time and space for her to get away.

Cat felt no guilt. As far as she was concerned, this was a dog eat dog world. The people who had died so that Cat could live were proof of her motto. If one of those fools had seized their chance and thrown her to the zombies before she could do it to them, that person would be standing here today instead of her. Since they hadn't, she had prospered and there would be no second chance in this life for any of the others.

Cat stretched and smiled. She was actually enjoying this new period of her life. She had found fresh strength and resolve since that day in school. She wasn't drifting along aimlessly. She was a survivor, one of the few with the courage and daring to flourish in these dark, deadly times. Where others had crumbled, she had stood firm and emerged a powerful, purposeful woman.

'No more maths for me,' she giggled, but softly, so as not to alert any zombies who might be sheltering in the shops around her.

But maybe it *wasn't* the end of her teaching days. Perhaps she could set up a survival school, teach other people how to thrive in this new, dangerous world.

She smiled again at the thought. Money wasn't worth anything now, but respect and admiration would be payment enough. She could also get her students to hunt for her, bring back food and drink, clothes and weapons. She liked it out here on the streets, but a day would come – not for a long time yet, but it paid to think in advance – when she would get old and slow. It might be a good idea to prepare for such a time as far ahead as possible.

Besides, if she surrounded herself with eager students, she would have lots of bodies to lob to the zombies if she got cornered.

Chuckling under her breath, wondering what she might name her school, Cat headed back to base. It was still early, but hungrier zombies sometimes came out while the sun was still in the sky. After Rule One – seize every chance in life – came Rule Two in the Cat Ward guidebook to surviving a zombie apocalypse — it doesn't pay to dawdle.

FIVE

Cat was staying in an old house in Muswell Hill. It had been deserted before the zombie attacks, the doors and windows on the ground floor all boarded over from the outside. She'd found a ladder in the back garden of a house a few streets away – you couldn't go into the hardware stores any more, as almost all of them were packed with EIY (eat it yourself) zombies – and used that to climb up and force open a window on the upper floor at the back of the house. The rooms were musty but clean, and she'd set up home there, maybe for a few days, maybe weeks — she'd decide as she went along.

Cat picked up the ladder where it was lying in the garden, set it against the wall and climbed. She knocked it over once she'd let herself in, as she always did. If zombies saw it standing there during the night, they'd investigate. They might be brain-dead beasts, but they weren't entirely clueless. You didn't have to be a genius to outwit them, but you couldn't underestimate them either.

In the morning, Cat would simply drop to the ground and go about her business. She was always careful to choose a room on a low floor. No penthouse apartments with spectacular views for her. The most important aspect of any home these days was that you were able to get out of it quickly and easily if you had to flee.

Cat laid out the goods that she had brought back – tins of food, a few bottles of water, a couple of sharp knives – then retired to a small bedroom. The windows weren't boarded over here, but there were heavy curtains on them.

Cat sat by the bedroom window, parted the curtains carefully, just enough to let through a crack of sunlight, then settled down and picked up one of the many books that were lying nearby. She read until the light faded completely, then set the book aside, let the curtain close and lay down for the night.

These were the worst hours, before sleep came, when there was nothing to do. There was a larger bedroom at the front of the house, and a street lamp shone outside it — though many of the lights in the city no longer worked, some still did. Cat could have gone in there and carried on reading. But she was afraid that a zombie would see her shadow moving. It was safer in the darkness.

She found herself thinking about her sister Jules and her family, her husband Paul and Cat's nephew George. They were the only people she really cared about. George had celebrated his eighth birthday just a week before everything went to hell, and Cat had helped organise his party. She often thought about that day, the fun she'd had, the way they'd all smiled as they posed for a photo together.

Cat had gone looking for her sister once she'd adjusted to life in a zombie-run world. She'd worked her way across to their house, spent several days in the neighbourhood, found some survivors and asked if they knew anything about Jules Bearman and her loved ones. Unfortunately, like so many others, they'd disappeared without trace, and while Cat hoped for the best – that they had escaped London and found shelter in a settlement outside the city – she feared the worst.

Cat would have liked to base herself in her sister's house, but that would have been dangerous. She had come across dozens of corpses in their homes during the course of her travels, people who had been overly attached to their possessions, who hadn't run when the chance presented itself.

Sentimentality was a weakness. Cat often rifled through the contents when she went through someone's house, figuring the dead had no right to privacy. She'd take anything that caught her fancy – jewellery, artwork, books – but she didn't hold on to anything for long, junking it before it could come to mean too much to her.

Cat took nothing from her sister's home, not even

the photo snapped on George's birthday. When it came time to flee – as it surely would – she didn't want to own anything she cared about. A person might pause in the middle of running away, to think about prized items that they were leaving behind, and pausing was bad. In this world of the living dead, it could be the death of you.

Cat didn't like thinking negatively so, in an attempt to drive away the dark thoughts, she started going through her plan for the next day, the streets she'd explore, the goods she would look for. Cat had moved all over London since escaping from school. She was taking the city a zone at a time, working her way through the boroughs.

In an ideal world, she would have settled in Knightsbridge, in a lovely mansion, where she could have dressed up in designer frocks and tiaras every day. But, although she'd made the most of the apoc- alypse and sampled the good life in some of London's finest neighbourhoods ('It's an ill wind that blows no one any good,' she sometimes giggled as she went to sleep in a four-poster bed), she never stayed in one place for long, and bedded down in kips as well as palaces. She'd spend a few days or weeks getting to know an area well and enjoying all that it had to offer, then move on before she grew complacent. No ties and no pattern — that was how Cat liked it.

When Cat tired of looking ahead, she cast her thoughts back, but not as far as George's party. Instead she recalled that day in the chemistry lab and all the days since, the three girls she had sacrificed, and the others who had followed.

Cat spent a long time remembering their faces and their expressions as she'd launched them at the zombies. It was cruel, but she found comfort in their distress. It made her feel strong, the fact that she had triumphed where they had fallen.

Stupid people, she thought. *They should have been sharper, faster, more cunning. I'm here and they're not, because I'm strong and they were weak. I'll never be weak like that. Never.*

Smiling grimly to herself, she drifted off to sleep, and the faces she saw in her dreams were the same faces she thought about when she was awake. Those faces were always with her, not because she couldn't shake them loose, but because she was determined to hold them tight. There would be no second chances in life for those dumb failures. She had seized her opportunities. They hadn't. They were zombie fodder, while she was a cold-hearted warrior who would do whatever it took to survive. If that meant becoming a monster, so be it. In a world of undead atrocities, Cat would choose abandoning her humanity and standing proudly among the monstrous every time. The alternative was a noble death, and to Cat Ward that was no sort of alternative at all.

SIX

Although Cat kept to herself most of the time, she had crossed paths with various groups since the city fell, survivors like her who had chosen to stay in London. She ran into another such group around Muswell Hill when she was out foraging, and although she was wary of them – London was a lawless place now, and some survivors were taking advantage of that, terrorising the living as well as the undead – she stopped to talk. You could sometimes pick up useful survival tips from those who were tough and resourceful.

There were eight people in the group, although one of those was a child, a young boy called Declan, who clung tightly to his mother Emma and didn't say a word.

The leader was a guy called Shaun. He was from Australia originally, and had learnt a lot about what it took to survive as a globetrotting thrill-seeker in the years before the zombies put paid to all such holiday activities.

'Don't you think you'd be better off with a partner or a gang like us?' Shaun asked. 'This is a hard place for loners. It's good when you have someone to watch your back.'

'The trouble is, I'd keep expecting them to stab me in it,' Cat said, and she was only half-joking. Since she didn't expect anyone to trust her – she'd throw them to the zombies in the blink of an eye to save her own neck – she could hardly bring herself to trust anybody else.

They traded stories and tips, warning each other about areas where there were lots of zombies. Sometimes Cat fed misinformation to people like this, sending them into zombie hot spots, figuring a zombie with a full stomach was one less she'd have to worry about for a while. But she liked Shaun – he was the sort of guy she would have picked for a boyfriend back in more innocent times – so she was straight with him.

At one point Shaun asked her if she'd heard the rumours about Stansted Airport. 'A few people have told me that the army has reclaimed the terminal,' he said. 'Apparently they're running flights out of there, importing recruits and equipment to use in the war with the living dead.'

'That sounds like a wild fantasy to me,' Cat snorted.

'Probably,' Shaun agreed, 'but I might go check it out if the rumours persist. I don't want anything to do with soldiers on the defensive – I think we've got a better chance of surviving here than in an army-run compound – but I plan to be part of the offensive when it starts in London. I want to be around for payback.'

They parted soon after that. Cat was half-tempted

to go with the group, but, if her feelings for Shaun deepened over time, she might one day stop to help him if they ran into trouble, rather than make a swift getaway. Shaun might be a good-looking, charming guy, but boyfriends were more trouble than they were worth these days. Cat chuckled — maybe they always had been!

Cat wasn't interested in payback – the zombies had set her free of the shackles of school and her old way of life, so she had nothing personal against them – but the rumours about Stansted and the army intrigued her. She found it hard to credit the stories, especially since she heard nothing about such a manoeuvre on the official radio station over the next few days, but her curiosity had been stimulated. If the rumours were true, she might be able to cut a deal with the soldiers, do some work for them and earn a flight out to a zombie-free island.

Cat had thought about leaving London and joining up with people in one of the army-run compounds in the countryside – not least because it would allow her to search afresh for Jules, Paul and

George – but she didn't like the idea of walling herself in. An island with no zombies was a different proposition. She could envisage herself settling back with a cocktail at sunset. It would be nicer than holing up in silence for the night.

So, even though it was a long shot, Cat headed east the next day, towards Tottenham Hale. It was a trek from Muswell Hill, at least a couple of hours if she moved as cautiously as she normally did, but she could get there and back easily before darkness fell.

She'd chosen Tottenham Hale because she knew that the railway line from central London to Stansted ran through the train station there. If she based herself in that part of the city, she could keep watch on the railway — if the airport was functional, the army might be using the line to move troops and supplies to and from it.

If Cat spotted soldiers on the line, she'd approach them and try to earn their trust. Failing that, she could hike all the way out to the airport. It would be long – probably a couple of days – and dangerous, but, after all this time on the streets, she fancied her chances.

But that was a job for another time. All she wanted to do right now was scout as far as the train station, see what shape that part of London was in. If she found it overrun with zombies, she'd withdraw to consider alternative routes. If, on the other hand, it looked quiet, she'd search for a suitable place to base herself, before moving her gear across over the coming days, so that she could start keeping watch on the line.

Cat wound her way east slowly and carefully. Some survivors kept to the main roads when they wandered, clear of the buildings. Many of them tried to mimic the movements of the undead, hoping to be mistaken for zombies if they were spotted by brain munchers.

It wasn't a bad method, but it wasn't Cat's way. She preferred to hug the buildings, creeping along in the shadows, ducking and sometimes even crawling under windows, darting past open doorways. The way she figured it, if you were in the middle of a road, there was a chance you might be spotted by several zombies in different places at the same time and, if a group came lumbering after you from various directions, it spelled trouble. Her way meant you weren't spotted as often, and you usually only had to worry about an assault from a single source when you were.

Cat hadn't had to fight with the undead many times, but was prepared for war if it found her. She carried a sword and a variety of long knives, two axes and a short spear which was strapped to her back. She wore gloves and a mask, to protect her from spraying zombie blood, which was as infectious as a bite or scratch.

Cat had a gun too, which she'd picked up a long time ago but never fired. The noise would probably bring loads of zombies running. She'd only use that in an emergency, as a last resort, or maybe turn it on herself if she was trapped with no way out.

Cat frowned at that thought and quickly pushed it away. She didn't like to contemplate worst-case scenarios. A survivor should focus on the positives, not the negatives. Let losers like those she'd thrown to the zombies worry about stuff like that. Cat had more important things to think about — like what cocktail she'd choose first if (*when*) she made it to her paradise island!

Smiling at that image, Cat paused to spray on more perfume – the undead responded to the scent of sweat, so she masked it as much as she could – then calmly pushed ahead, ready for whatever the city had to throw at her.

SEVEN

It was an unremarkable journey until she got to Seven Sisters. She only had a single run-in with a zombie. He had been lying in the doorway of a pet shop, an elderly man whose legs didn't work.

The zombie spotted her coming and dragged himself forward, eager to grab her ankles and haul himself up to bite into her brain. It was no contest. She'd simply stood her ground, shifted slightly to the left as he drew near and used her spear to impale his brain. After he'd stopped shuddering, she pulled out the spear, cautiously wiped it clean of any dangerously infectious bits of zombie brain and carried on as normal.

There was a large junction outside Seven Sisters Tube station, where she paused to apply more perfume and have a sip of water. An uneasy feeling crept over Cat as she was drinking, an itch at the back of her skull. It was probably nothing, but she'd learnt to pay attention to her instincts. It was better to react to a false alarm a dozen times than get caught out once.

Cat stepped out of the shadows and moved into the middle of the junction. She was a target now, but it meant she had a clear view in all directions. She turned slowly, fingers flexing. She couldn't see anything, but that itch was still there, so she held her ground and drew her sword from its scabbard.

All was silent for several minutes. Although she still felt uneasy, Cat figured she'd waited long enough. If something bad was going to happen, it should have happened by now.

Still, she decided to cut short her exploration. Better to retreat and come back another time. She wasn't going to ignore a warning, even if there was nothing to actually be wary of. She'd return to her base in Muswell Hill, rest up for the night, come back again tomorrow, but this time a different way. If she got the bad feeling again, she'd look for a different route to Stansted.

Cat began to retrace her steps. She'd covered no more than a few metres when a whistle suddenly rang out, a high, piercing note.

Cat froze, her eyes widening, trying to place the source of the sound. But it was impossible to tell where it had come from. As she waited for it to come again, she spotted movement on the road ahead of her. Her stomach shrank as several zombies lumbered into view, caught sight of her and picked up their pace.

Cat turned to race south, but there were more zombies that way. She spared just enough time for a single, foul curse. Then she about-turned and headed north at top speed, up Tottenham High Road, the zombies in hot pursuit.

EIGHT

Cat was desperate to get off the High Road. She guessed there would be hundreds of zombies littering the shops, restaurants, cafés and pubs along it. They would surely spot her and spill out to join the hunt.

The problem was there were zombies down every side street that she came to, a small pack in each. As soon as they saw her, they started forward, moaning hungrily and gnashing their fangs. It would have been suicide to try to slip past them on the small, tight streets.

Cat couldn't understand what was happening. You

got the occasional undead straggler outside in the daytime, but nothing like this. Also, it was bizarre how they were in every street, and always at the far end, not close enough to dart out and grab her.

At least the buildings on either side of the road appeared to be clear. Or, if there were zombies inside, they were resting away from the doors and windows, unaware of what was happening outside.

Cat ran at a steady pace. She tried not to pant or surrender to panic. She was in a bad spot, but it had been worse in the school and she'd got out of there alive. She had to keep her head, stay focused, search for a way out.

She thought about ducking into a shop or pub and barricading herself in, then looking for an escape route out back. But that would be a serious gamble. There were dozens of zombies chasing her. It wouldn't take them long to tear through any barrier that she might set in their path. And if she wound up in a building with no back door . . .

No, it was better to keep running. At first she counted the side streets, but lost track pretty quickly.

There seemed to be an endless number of them, and every one was blocked off by zombies.

She heard a few more whistles as she fled. They confused her. She didn't know who was making the noises. If it had been just the one, she'd have assumed it came from a zombie who had swallowed a whistle at some point. But the sounds came from different places, behind, ahead and to either side of her.

The whistles actually scared Cat more than the zombies. She felt confident that she could outpace the living dead and lose them once she got off the High Road, but the whistles were an unknown factor.

Perhaps they were the work of soldiers. Maybe survivors like her were clearing out this area and herding zombies ahead of them. That would explain why the undead were coming from all over the place. She had heard of the army doing this in towns around the country, reclaiming them for the living. Maybe this was their first such venture in London.

Cat would have been delighted to learn of such an operation any other time, but right now she was caught in the middle of the rush and that was bad news. Because, if the people with the whistles were directing the zombies towards a dead end where they could be picked off by snipers or scorched with flame-throwers, there would be no way for them to tell Cat apart from the monsters they had targeted.

Cat was certain that if she didn't make it off the High Road within the next few minutes she'd be as damned as those who were trailing along behind her. But, with nowhere to turn, she had no choice but to keep going as she was and run.

NINE

Cat's legs were starting to tire as she drew close to Tottenham Hotspur football stadium. She had worked out a lot more these last few months than she ever had before, and was in the best condition of her life, but she'd never had to endure a sustained sprint like this. She could have jogged for hours without pause, but the zombies were running, not jogging, so she had to match their pace.

The undead were slower than they'd been in life, lacking the fluid coordination of the living. But since they didn't use their lungs, they didn't get tired the way humans did. They could maintain this speed indefinitely, whereas Cat was quickly running out of steam.

She was worrying about that as she drew abreast of the stadium, but that worry was swiftly wiped away when she saw another horde of zombies coming at her from the top end of the High Road.

Cat drew to a fearful halt and stared at the advancing zombies. She glanced over her shoulder — there was an army of the undead behind her, closing in. A quick look left and right — more zombies racing at her from the side streets.

She was caught in the middle, no way out.

Cat pulled down her mask and started to moan, a long, loud wailing sound. How could this have happened? She was always so careful. If soldiers were at large, shepherding the zombies into a kill zone, she should have spotted the signs. She wasn't blind, deaf or stupid.

As zombies closed in on her from all sides, Cat stopped moaning. If this was to be her finale, so be it. She drew her gun, gazed at it glumly, then got ready to rid the zombies of their chance to kill her.

Before Cat could raise the gun, a whistle blew, sharp and sustained. She looked around with surprise. This time the blast had come from a place much closer to her, within the net of encroaching zombies. But she couldn't see anyone.

Then she spotted an opening into the stadium. All of the turnstiles, which fans of the club had passed through over the decades, had been blocked off with heavy steel doors, but there was one exception. A single door, close to where she was standing, hung ajar.

Cat couldn't be sure that the whistle had come from there. And she had no idea what lay beyond — maybe the corridor was home to even more zombies than those chasing her out here. If she ducked inside and slammed the door shut, and the stadium turned out to be infested with the living dead, she was damned.

But what other choice did she have? This was a chance to get away, and she had dedicated her whole life, especially since the zombie outbreak, to seizing every chance that came her way.

So, putting her gun away, Cat raced for the door. She nearly didn't make it – the zombies up the side street almost beat her to the punch – but she swung in just ahead of her savage hunters. Grabbing hold of the heavy door, she heaved with all her strength and it began to swing shut.

One of the zombies got to the door before it could close and slipped a hand through the gap. The door jammed on the foul creature's forearm. If Cat had hesitated, the others would have been able to slide their own hands in and force the door open, and the game would have been lost.

But it had been a long time since Cat Ward hesitated. Sliding free a knife, she lashed out at the hand and cut it clean off at the wrist. The fingers twitched wildly as the hand dropped. Cat kicked the hand away – the kick would have drawn admiring comments if she'd done it on the pitch in the old days – then slammed the door shut. There were several bolts, and she slotted them all home, one after the other, in rapid succession, like a machine.

She heard the zombies howling and thumping on

the door, but it held and, as she stepped back from it, shivering and gasping, she realised with surprise and delight that she had made it. They couldn't get to her now. She was safe.

Cat whooped and punched the air. She couldn't believe it. That had been so close. For a second there she was sure that she was doomed.

Then a whistle sounded in the corridor behind her and, as Cat fell silent again and slowly turned to face the gloom of the unknown, she had to concede to herself that maybe she had celebrated too soon.

All of the zombies appeared to be locked outside the stadium.

But what was locked inside here with her?

TEN

Cat lowered her mask and nearly called out, 'Hello?'
But that would have given her away. She figured
there was a very good chance that the person with the
whistle already knew that she was here, but it would
be foolish to draw their attention, just in case they
were unaware of her presence.

She told herself that she might be worrying about
nothing. Maybe this place was packed with living soldiers, waiting to rain down hell on the zombies outside
the stadium. They'd be surprised when they saw her.
She'd tell them her story and they'd commend her on

her narrow escape, invite her to leave with them when they departed.

But that bad feeling was back. Her scalp was itching like crazy. This felt wrong on every level. She had no idea what was waiting for her up ahead, but she was almost a hundred per cent positive that it wasn't a squad of soldiers.

Cat stood there for a while, listening to the zombies pound on the door, getting her breath back, recovering her poise. She cleaned the knife automatically and put it away. She thought about drawing the gun again, but she didn't want to provoke an attack — if there were soldiers here, and they saw someone advancing with a gun, they might open fire defensively. Better to advance unarmed until she knew what she was dealing with.

When Cat was back to normal, she looked around. Her eyes had adjusted to the gloom, but there wasn't much to see, just the concrete walls of the corridor. There were lights overhead, but they were switched off.

The tunnel ran straight ahead of her, then turned

to the right. Cat took a deep breath and walked to the turning. She stuck her head round the corner slowly, not sure what to expect. But all she found was another stretch of corridor.

Cat glanced back longingly at the door. She almost wanted to open it and throw herself into the arms of the zombies. At least she knew what would happen to her if she did that.

But suicide was not an option for the determined Cat Ward. And her imagination would only run riot if she stood here and waited — in her experience, there were no worse horrors than those you could dream up inside your own head when you were scared and had too much time to think.

So, with another deep breath, Cat turned the corner and set off deeper into the heart of the stadium, surrendering herself to the mysterious, menacing vagaries of the maze.

ELEVEN

The corridor kept twisting and turning. She came to a variety of junctions. A small arrow had been scratched into one of the walls at each juncture, indicating the way forward. The arrows did nothing to make Cat feel any calmer — if anything, they set her nerves even more on edge. She thought about ignoring them and taking the opposite direction, but then she might get lost. At least if she followed the path of the arrows, she could easily backtrack at any point.

She passed several doors that were locked, but the handle of one finally turned when she tried it.

Cat paused. What if there was a team of zombie footballers behind the door? Maybe the players had been turned and ended up trapped in a changing room. The whistle she'd heard might have been an undead referee blowing for the start of a match. If she opened this door, a team of hungry players might storm out, cut her head open, tuck into her brain, then head on out to the pitch for a game that would never kick off.

'The hell with it,' Cat muttered with a shaky grin. 'It was always my dream to end up in the arms of a professional footballer with loads of money.'

She pushed the door open and braced herself for the rush.

Nothing happened.

After a few seconds, Cat stepped forward. There was a light switch on the wall. When she tried it, the light overhead flickered on, revealing a bare, dusty room. There were a few boots here and there, some bandages, a crusty old towel. But no footballers, alive or undead.

Cat turned off the light – energy conscious even in

these chaotic times – and carried on along the corridor. She came to a few more doors, some of which were open, but the rooms were all as empty as the first one had been.

She spotted a whistle on the floor of one room and stared at it suspiciously. There was no way to tell if this was an ancient piece of equipment or the whistle that had lured her into this place. She bent over to pick it up, meaning to try it, then stopped with her fingers outstretched. If the whistle had been blown by a zombie, its germs would be smeared across the mouthpiece. If she put it to her lips, she'd be infected immediately and would turn into one of the brain-hungry monsters within a minute or two.

Cat scowled and withdrew her hand. She needed to be more careful. She had almost walked straight into potential disaster. That wasn't like her. She was obviously more spooked than she had admitted.

Stepping back out into the corridor, Cat gave herself a few moments to breathe and relax. 'Come on,' she whispered. 'You've faced worse than this. Don't lose your nerve now. Whatever's going on, you can deal with it.'

The little pep talk worked and she walked more steadily after that. She ignored the rest of the doors that she came to, marching with a purpose now, determined to get to the pitch and find out what was waiting for her there.

She arrived at the tunnel opening a few minutes later. Daylight was streaming through it, a welcome sight after the dimness of the corridors. Cat felt like running out into it, but she didn't. Composure was the key here.

Edging forward, she moved to the side, keeping to the shadows. She was expecting zombies or soldiers, but, as she came to the mouth of the tunnel and caught sight of the pitch, her jaw dropped. She stood there in disbelief, then stepped out in a daze and said very softly, with no idea that she was speaking, 'No bloody way!'

TWELVE

A massive circus tent had been erected in the middle of the pitch. An old-style big top, a mix of red and yellow stripes. There were four peaks in the billowing roof, a big flag flying from each, bunting running from the spikes to the ground.

There was a large, framed entrance. An awning swept down over it and there was a painted sign above that. As Cat stumbled forward, hardly able to believe her eyes, the text on the sign came into focus.

MR DOWLING'S EMPORIUM
OF WONDERS

The words meant nothing to Cat, but they made her shiver regardless, because she could see now that they had been painted with blood.

Fresh blood, still dripping slowly down the canvas.

There was a low, steady growling noise behind her. It had been there all along and Cat had mistaken it for a natural hum, an electrical generator or something like that. But, as she paused and stared at the sign, she realised this was like no other hum she had ever heard.

With a horrible, sick feeling, Cat forced herself to turn and look at the rest of the stadium. She'd assumed it would be abandoned, but to her shock and dismay she saw that every seat was taken.

By a zombie.

Cat's head spun. She had no idea how many people the stadium could hold, but figured it must be at least thirty or forty thousand. She couldn't see a spare seat anywhere she looked. Every single one was occupied by a member of the living dead, men, women and children. She'd never seen so many zombies in one place before. And they were all sitting still, just growling and staring ... at *her*.

Cat didn't know how so many had gathered together, or why they were seated like that. All she knew was that she had to get out of here, and quick.

She took a frantic step back towards the mouth of the tunnel. As soon as she did that, every zombie leapt to its feet. There was an audible crack in the air as they all stood at the same time and glared. The noise of the growling rose sharply.

Cat gulped and stepped away from the tunnel. The zombies slowly sank back into their seats, the growl settling into its low rhythmic hum again.

Cat started to cry. It had been a long time since she'd shed tears, but this had shaken her like nothing else. It wasn't just the fact that there were so many of them and that they could surge forward and take her in the blink of an eye. It was the way they were behaving. Zombies didn't act like this. Something was wrong here, wrong in a way that nothing had ever been wrong for Cat before.

For a few minutes she could only stand there, sobbing, wanting to run but too afraid to move.

But because Cat was made of stern stuff she

eventually wiped away the tears and took stock. The zombies were still sitting and watching her. She could see that some of them were drooling, licking their lips at the thought of digging into her fresh, hot brain. But for some reason they held back.

Cat didn't know what was going on, but she knew the only way was forward, into the tent. If she tried to retreat, the living dead would attack. She hated playing into the hands of whoever it was that had set this up, but she had no option. Nobody could argue with tens of thousands of zombies.

Turning her back on the stands, shivering uncontrollably, Cat Ward faced the big top and read the ominous sign again. She had no idea who Mr Dowling was, or what might be stored in his emporium of wonders.

But she knew she was about to find out.

Sniffing miserably, wiping the last of the tears away, Cat lowered her head, took the deepest, shakiest breath of her life and started forward into the gigantic, hellish, red and yellow tent.

THIRTEEN

There was a noticeable drop in temperature as soon as Cat stepped beneath the awning. She stopped there for a while, peering ahead. There were curtains ahead of her, so she couldn't see past the entrance. She thought about waiting here, but what good would that achieve? The zombies weren't going to leave, and it wasn't like she could slip off during the night when they were asleep — the undead had no need for sleep, and the hours of the night were theirs.

As Cat hesitated, torn between advancing and turning back to try to make a break for the tunnel, the curtains suddenly parted and a man stepped through.

'Come on,' he snapped. 'We don't have all day. It doesn't pay to keep Mr Dowling waiting.'

Cat gawped at the man. He was like nobody she had ever seen, not even the decaying zombies. His skin was a mess, purple in places, covered with pus-filled sores. In some areas, strips of it were peeling away. He had limp grey hair and eerie yellow eyes. Some of his teeth were missing and the rest were black and rotting. Cat could smell the stench of his breath even this far away. He was wearing a tatty hoodie, but the hood was pushed back to reveal his face.

'What's the matter?' the man smirked. 'Never seen a mutant before?'

'What . . . are you?' Cat croaked.

'The last person you'll ever see if you don't get a move on,' he huffed. When Cat just shook her head and stared wide-eyed, he sighed impatiently. 'The name's Kinslow. I'm your usher for the day. Come with me and I'll show you to your seat.'

'Seat?' Cat echoed weakly, looking back at the zombies in the stands.

'Not up there,' Kinslow chuckled. 'This is a seat inside. Come on,' he said again, leaning forward this time and extending a hand to her. 'You don't want to miss the show, do you?'

'Are you infectious?' Cat asked, eyeing the hand uneasily.

'No,' Kinslow said. 'You're safe as houses with me.'

Cat licked her lips, started to stretch out a hand, stopped. 'I want to go home,' she whimpered.

'I know,' Kinslow said kindly. Then his features hardened. 'But this isn't a time for going home. It's a time for doing what Mr Dowling tells you to do. And he wants you to come and see the show.'

'Who is he?' Cat wheezed. 'What does he want with me? How did you get the zombies to chase me here? You did, didn't you? You controlled them with the whistles and had them chase me up the High Road.'

'Not me personally,' Kinslow said. 'But people like me, yeah.' He clicked his fingers. 'You'll find more answers inside, but I'm not gonna wait for you for-ever. Come with me now or I'll leave you here for the zombies.'

Cat shuddered, then steeled herself and took Kinslow's hand. He tutted when he realised she was wearing gloves and quickly peeled them off. Cat didn't protest as he tossed them away, before taking her hand again. His palm was warmer than she had anticipated, but sticky with dried pus.

'Will I be OK in there?' she asked as he led her forward and pushed aside the curtains.

'With Mr Dowling to look after you?' Kinslow replied with a friendly purr. He shook his head and the purr turned into a wicked cackle. 'I doubt it!'

FOURTEEN

It looked for the most part like a normal circus. A sawdust-strewn ring in the centre, encircled by a low barrier and surrounded by rows of seats, a couple of trapezes and a high wire overhead.

But there were no normal people in the capacity crowd, no excited children with candyfloss and balloons, no bored dads or chattering mums. Instead the seats were filled with mutants like Kinslow and nightmarish babies.

Cat had expected the mutants – Kinslow had told her outside that there were others like him – but the babies caught her off guard. They all looked the same and were dressed in similar white gowns. They had large eyes that were entirely white, and sharp little fangs that flashed when they smiled or scowled.

The babies were sitting up like adults, hands on their knees, watching a clown cavort in the ring. They didn't applaud or laugh at his antics, but made soft cooing noises. If Cat had shut her eyes, she could almost have believed that she was in an aviary.

Kinslow led Cat forward to a throne by the ringside. The throne didn't belong here. It must have been stolen from a palace. It was huge and ornate, layered in gold, studded with diamonds. It made a big impression on Cat, even in the midst of her terror and confusion, and she wondered how much such an elaborate chair would have cost in the old days.

'It's not to my taste, but Mr Dowling loves a bit of bling,' Kinslow grinned.

Cat didn't reply. She was still staring round the tent at the babies and mutants. Her legs felt weak and she had begun to hope that she was dreaming. She'd become accustomed to the world of zombies, but this was a whole new realm. Perhaps it was all nothing more than a freakish nightmare.

'Are you real?' Cat whispered, the question going out not just to Kinslow, but to his fellow mutants and the scores of cooing babies.

'As real as anything in this crazy, mixed-up world,' Kinslow laughed. 'Do you want me to pinch you to prove it?' He was still holding Cat's hand, and now he squeezed sharply, causing her to cry out with pain and jerk her fingers free.

'Don't do that again,' Cat snapped as he reached for her.

'Or what?' Kinslow smirked.

'Or I'll draw my sword and chop your ugly head off.'

Kinslow pursed his lips, impressed by the threat. 'You'd suffer for it if you harmed me,' he told her.

'Sure,' she sneered, forgetting her fear for a moment. 'But that wouldn't do you any good, would it? Beheading won't stop a zombie, but I think it would mean the end of the likes of you.'

Kinslow nodded sombrely. Then he smiled again.

'You're a gutsy woman, Miss Ward. That's why you're here. Mr Dowling admires ruthless determination. He wants to give you a chance to shine.'

'Who is this Mr Dowling?' Cat growled. 'Where is he?'

'Why, I thought you already knew,' Kinslow said. 'He's right there.'

He pointed to the clown in the circus ring and, as Cat's eyes settled on the strange performer, she quickly realised that the zombies, mutants and babies were small fry on the weirdness scale when compared with the brain-chillingly macabre ringmaster at the heart of this insane show.

FIFTEEN

Mr Dowling was wearing a pinstriped suit inlaid with colourful patches. A severed face dangled from either shoulder. Guts were wrapped round his arms like snakes, while ears were pinned to the legs of his trousers. He wore large red shoes and a tiny skull was attached to the end of each. Cat wasn't sure if the skulls had come from babies like those in the audience or from human infants.

The clown's wild hair was a collection of strands which had been harvested from the heads of various people and stapled into his scalp. He had painted his face white and his lips a dark blue colour. The flesh had been carved away around his eyes and filled in with soot, while v-shaped channels had been cut out of his cheeks and the bone beneath dyed pink.

In a final surreal touch, an eyeball had been stuck to the end of his nose and decorated with small red stars.

Mr Dowling's eyes swivelled madly from one side of their sockets to the other as he made his way towards the petrified Cat. His skin rippled and his lips twitched. A badge with his name on it was pinned to the lapel of his coat.

Cat tried to pull away as Mr Dowling reached out to stroke her cheek, but Kinslow held her in place. The clown's fingers were cold and Cat could see that much of the flesh had been sliced away from them, exposing bones, veins and arteries.

Mr Dowling made a curious choking noise, then opened his mouth. A death's-head moth was relaxing on his tongue. As Cat gawped, the moth spread its wings and took flight. It fluttered around in front of her eyes and she thought for a moment that it would land on her nose. But then it started to rise into the air above her.

Before the moth could get clear, the clown clapped his hands and smashed it to a pulp. He smeared the remains of the moth over his lips, then leant forward and kissed Cat quickly.

Cat squealed and pushed Mr Dowling away, then spat out bits of moth and wiped her tongue with the palm of her hand, trying to get rid of the horrible taste.

'How beautiful,' Kinslow sighed. 'He's a poet and a lover.'

'What sort of a freak is he?' Cat moaned.

'He's the emperor here,' Kinslow said stiffly, 'and you'd do well to pay him the respect he's due, or he'll toss you to the zombies and give them the all-clear to cut loose on you.'

Cat shivered but said nothing. Mr Dowling looked her up and down. At least she thought that's what he was doing. It was hard to tell, because of the way his eyes danced around so much.

Mr Dowling hopped up on to the throne and

made a shrill noise. Kinslow said, 'He wants you to sit on his lap.'

'You're joking,' Cat said weakly.

'I'm not a clown,' Kinslow sniffed. 'I don't bother with jokes.'

'But . . . how can you be sure?' she asked.

'He speaks to me,' Kinslow said, tapping the side of his head. 'Up here.'

'He's telepathic?' Cat was sceptical. 'I don't believe in telepathy.'

'Mr Dowling doesn't care about your beliefs,' Kinslow said harshly. 'Hop up on his lap before he loses patience.'

Cat cringed but forced herself to slide forward, into the clown's lap. He made another odd noise and wrapped his bony arms round her.

'He says you're a perfect fit,' Kinslow laughed.

'What now?' Cat asked nervously.

'Now . . .' Kinslow said dramatically and clicked his fingers. The lights around the tent snapped off, plunging everything into darkness. 'It's show time!'

SIXTEEN

Three spotlights were switched on and trained on the ring. A flashily dressed mutant was standing there — he must have darted forward during the blackout. Mr Dowling waved a hand at him and made a high-pitched squeaking noise.

'Up first,' Kinslow translated, 'we have Jaundice Jack, the world's number-one undead juggler.'

'But he's not undead,' Cat frowned. 'He's a mutant like you.'

'It will all become clear in a minute,' Kinslow promised.

As Cat watched, five zombies were led into the ring by a young mutant, a girl not much older than the students Cat used to teach. She was using a whistle to direct the zombies, who marched along listlessly. The mutants started chanting, 'Claudia! Claudia!' The girl smiled and waved to them, then scowled and blew her whistle again, keeping firm control over her charges.

When the zombies were standing still, Mr Dowling shoved Cat off his lap and stood up abruptly. Cat landed with a startled yelp and glared at the clown as he bounded past her into the ring.

Mr Dowling was halfway to the zombies when he stopped, pretended to slap his head, then ran back to Cat. He shook a hand at her and made a gibberish noise.

'He wants your sword,' Kinslow said.

'What for?' Cat asked.

'Does it matter?' Kinslow yawned. 'Just give him what he wants before he takes it by force.'

Cat felt uneasy, but drew her sword and handed it to the clown. She felt the bulge of her gun as she was removing the sword, and thought about taking it out and opening fire on Mr Dowling, but Kinslow was watching her intently and she didn't think she'd get very far.

Mr Dowling took the sword with a sweeping bow, then bounded over to the zombies. Without slowing down, he swung the sword and chopped off the head of the first zombie, then the second, the third, the fourth and the fifth. It happened so swiftly that the zombies didn't have time to react.

As Mr Dowling chopped off the last zombie's head, he pirouetted wildly, jumped into the air and landed on both knees, throwing away the sword and spreading his arms wide.

'Ta-dah!' Kinslow shouted, and all of the other mutants cheered.

Mr Dowling hopped to his feet and returned to his throne. Settling down, he patted his lap and Cat reluctantly climbed back up again.

Inside the ring, the bodies of the zombies were staggering around. They didn't need their heads to survive, but they were directionless without them.

The mutants laughed and shouted rude jokes at the undead victims. Cat didn't feel any pity for the zombies. She was as scornful of them as the mutants were, and laughed as one woman tripped over her own head and fell.

The mutant who had been introduced as Jaundice Jack moved between the zombies as they flailed around. He picked up one head, then another, then a third. Facing the audience, he nodded, and from somewhere beneath the seats a band struck up a low, slow tune.

Jaundice Jack listened to the music for a time, then threw one of the heads up into the air. As it soared high, he tossed up the second head, then the third, and in the twinkling of an eye he was juggling the three severed heads.

'I get it now,' Cat smiled. 'He's not undead, but he juggles the undead.'

Kinslow didn't bother to comment on that.

Jaundice Jack kicked the heads of the fourth and fifth zombies up from the ground into the air, and added them seamlessly to the mix, so that he was now juggling all five at the same time. It was a difficult procedure, more so than it would have been with inanimate objects, because the jaws of the zombies still worked and they bit at the mutant's fingers as he juggled.

Jaundice Jack juggled the heads for a couple of minutes, then called for some assistance from the crowd. At his summons, a couple of the babies came forward carrying a large, empty ice-cream cone. They positioned themselves close to Jaundice Jack and waited. He checked that they were in place, then nodded at the crowd.

'Three! Two! One!' the mutants hooted.

As the countdown concluded, Jaundice Jack launched one of the heads high into the air. The babies ran around comically, tilting the cone this way and that, then caught the head as it fell. The crowd cheered as the babies ran with the grisly cranial scoop towards the side of the ring. Once there, they lobbed the head into the middle of a pack of mutants, who lashed at it with clubs, hammers and axes which they'd been keeping down by their sides. The brain was destroyed and the zombie's body dropped inside the ring, lifeless forever now.

Jaundice Jack and the babies disposed of the other four heads in a similar way, before leaving the ring to huge applause. Cat was one of those who was clapping with delight. She had chanted along in the countdowns too. She fully approved of killing zombies, and for a while had forgotten the trouble she was in.

'Enjoying it?' Kinslow smirked.

'Yes,' Cat said, her eyes wide and bright.

'Well, hold tight, sweetcake,' he winked. 'You ain't seen nothing yet!'

SEVENTEEN

'Next up we have trapeze artists,' Kinslow said after a short break while the bodies were being cleared from the ring.

A dozen zombies in spandex costumes were led forward and lured up rope ladders on opposite sides of the big top by a pair of whistle-blowing mutants — the girl called Claudia and a man.

'These were all skilled performers in life,' Kinslow explained to Cat. 'It took us ages to track them down. We want to see how they fare in death, if they can do what they did when they were alive.'

'I doubt they can,' Cat said.

'Probably not,' Kinslow agreed. 'But it'll be fun to find out.'

When the undead trapeze artists were in place, the mutant to Cat's left directed the first of them towards the trapeze and placed it in the zombie's hand. The zombie did nothing, just stared at the trapeze cluelessly. At a grunt from Mr Dowling, the mutant pushed the zombie forward.

The trapeze artist didn't get very far before losing his grip and crashing to the ground, where he mewled with pain as bones snapped all over his body.

To Cat's right, Claudia set the first of her performers in motion, and this one fared no better than the first.

The third actually held on for a while and swung gracefully back and forth. Then, as a dim memory kicked in, he let go and tried to do a somersault. He fell more heavily than the first two and landed on his head, which shattered like a melon, destroying his brain and ending his life. But he received a standing ovation from the mutants, who appreciated the effort.

After another abject failure, the mutants on the platforms set two of the trapeze artists off at the same time. They clashed mid-air and fell in a tangled heap. The next pair followed suit, but the last two performed more admirably. As they soared towards one another, the one to Cat's right let go of its bar and reached out to the zombie to her left.

Since the second zombie was still clinging to his bar, he wasn't able to catch the first one, who landed in a broken mess on the hard floor of the tent. But he kept swinging and, as he sailed from one side to the other, he pulled himself up, locked his legs round the bar, then hung down and stretched out his arms to catch a fellow performer who was no longer there.

The mutants fell silent as they watched the lone, lonely zombie swinging in the air, reaching out towards a forever absent partner.

'It's sad,' Kinslow muttered.

'No it's not,' Cat snorted. 'It's ridiculous.'

'You don't feel any sympathy for him?' Kinslow scowled.

'He's a brain-eating monstrosity,' Cat snarled. 'Pity is wasted on the likes of him.'

'Maybe,' Kinslow shrugged as the mutant on the platform hauled in the zombie and helped him from the trapeze, before leading him back down the rope ladder to be set free. 'But those who can't find pity within themselves for the lost can hardly expect to be granted any when their own time of judgement comes.'

'What do you mean?' Cat snapped, frightened by the mutant's cold tone.

'Hush,' Kinslow said in response. 'Here comes the next act. And this one's a doozy.'

EIGHTEEN

An overweight zombie was led forward by Claudia – the crowd chanted her name again, but she ignored them this time – and announced by Kinslow as a fire-eater. When the zombie was centre stage, a mutant in a chef's hat and apron came out, pushing a large pot on wheels. The chef stopped a few metres away from the zombie and waited while Claudia tied her charge's hands behind his back. When all was ready, the chef opened up the pot to reveal a tray filled with small chunks.

Cat immediately clocked the chunks as bits of

brain. She'd seen enough over the past months to recognise them from a long way off.

The zombie began to moan hungrily. He staggered towards the pot, but stopped when Claudia tooted sharply on her whistle. Cat could see that he was torn, but obedience to the girl took precedence over his desire to tuck in.

As the zombie wavered, the mutant by the pot produced a can and soaked the slivers of brain in an acrid liquid. Cat couldn't place the scent, but it made her nose twitch and her eyes water. Mr Dowling on the other hand loved it, and he began swaying beneath her, almost throwing her off as he licked his lips and moved jerkily from one side of the throne to the other.

The chef waited a couple of minutes while the band played a fast-paced song. Then he dug a book of matches out of a pocket, lit one, let the flame strengthen and tossed it on to the brains, instantly igniting the grey, juicy scraps.

'That's an eternal flame,' Kinslow snickered. 'It will burn until the brain has been entirely consumed, even if you douse it in water.'

Using a long-handled fork, the mutant picked up a piece of the flaming brains and walked round the bound zombie. The zombie's gaze fastened on the fiery morsel and he drooled as the chef teased him with it, waving it under his nose and luring him forward, almost to the edge of the ring, where Mr Dowling was eagerly watching.

Finally, at a nod from the clown, the mutant threw the piece of brain up into the air. Claudia blew her whistle and the zombie made a happy moaning noise. Opening his mouth, he moved beneath the now falling bit of brain, caught it between his teeth and swallowed it whole.

The mutant with the fork returned to the pot and started lobbing more burning scraps into the air. The zombie caught them all, whirling around like a dervish, gulping each piece down. He was wincing from the pain of the fire, but he kept on eating, hunger getting the better of his agony.

After a while, the zombie's stomach wall started to glow beneath his shirt. As Cat watched with fascination, flames erupted from his flesh, burning the shirt away and spreading across his chest. Soon he was a giant ball of fire, but still he went on snapping at the fresh bits of brain that were thrown his way.

'Hot stuff,' Kinslow grinned tightly, watching Cat for her reaction.

'Have you got any marshmallows for me to toast?' she sniffed.

'You don't feel sorry for him?' Kinslow asked.

'Should I?' she shrugged.

'I suppose not,' Kinslow sighed as the flames reached the zombie's brain and ate into it, finally extinguishing his spark of reanimation. 'But maybe the next act will stir you.' He leant in close and whispered in her ear with relish, 'The human cannonball!'

NINETEEN

A giant cannon was wheeled into the ring by a group of sweating mutants. Excited murmurs ran through the crowd and Cat got the sense that this was going to be the highlight of the show. She sat up straight, eyes bright, looking forward to whatever ghoulish treat the imaginative mutants had lined up next.

Once the cannon was in place, other mutants who had been standing by the far side of the tent tugged on ropes and a panel of canvas in the roof was pulled clear, creating a hole. Cat could see through the hole into the stadium outside, where the zombies were still sitting patiently in the stands.

Cat was expecting random undead victims to be shot from the cannon, but instead three living humans were herded into the ring — a man, a woman and a boy of eight years old. Cat knew that he was eight, because she'd bought him a birthday card with that number on it earlier in the year.

'Behold the Bearmans,' Kinslow told her as the terrified trio were stopped by the cannon's base. 'Mr Dowling has been holding them back for a special occasion.'

Cat moaned softly and shook her head, fresh tears spilling down her cheeks, her impish joy giving way to genuine horror.

'What's wrong?' Kinslow gasped, feigning surprise. 'You don't know these people, do you?'

'Please,' Cat sobbed, clutching Mr Dowling and appealing to the clown for mercy. 'Please don't hurt them. They haven't done anything wrong. Please.'

Mr Dowling stared at her seriously for a long moment. Then he burped.

Kinslow laughed with vicious delight. 'Oh, that's right, I almost forgot. It's your sister, her husband and child. I bet you didn't expect to be reunited with them like this.'

Cat had never truly expected to see Jules, Paul and George Bearman again.

And now she wished she hadn't.

'How?' Cat cried as the mutants forced her brother-in-law Paul up into the mouth of the cannon. 'How did you find them?'

'We have ways and means,' Kinslow purred.

'Let them go,' Cat begged. 'Please.'

'No can do,' Kinslow smiled, then pressed a finger to her lips to shush her.

Claudia was operating the cannon. As Kinslow silenced the horrified Cat, the girl called to the crowd to begin the countdown.

'Three! Two! One!' the mutants shouted.

The cannon was fired and Paul went flying through the air ... out through the hole in the roof ... to land among the hungry, eager zombies in the stands.

Cat saw a ripple run through the area where Paul landed, as zombies bunched round him and tore in. Seconds later they settled back and Cat could almost hear the munching sounds as the lucky few tucked into fresh, hot chunks of Paul Bearman's brain.

Cat shut her eyes and cursed.

'Nuh-uh,' Kinslow said, pinching her chin. 'We won't continue until you look. We can wait all day and night if we have to.'

'I won't look,' Cat said. 'Not unless you let Jules and George go.'

'If you don't look,' Kinslow responded, 'then we'll torture them before we fire them from the cannon.'

Cat's eyes automatically snapped open and she stared at the mutant, appalled. 'Why are you doing this to me?' she croaked.

'I'll tell you soon,' Kinslow promised. 'First, Mr Dowling wants to get involved.'

The clown leapt to his feet, throwing Cat to the ground again. He hurried forward, humming an out-of-tune song. The mutants in the ring were now forcing Jules to climb up into the cannon. George, her little boy, was screaming and reaching out to pull her back, but the mutants were holding him down. Jules was sobbing, yelling out George's name, telling him to be brave, it was all going to be OK, there was a net outside and they would all be fine.

Cat wanted to call to her sister, but she felt too ashamed. She knew they were here because of her. She had no idea why the clown and his mutants were interested in her, but they had obviously targeted her for some sick reason, and her sister's family were paying the price for their link to her. It was enough to remind Cat of her humanity for the first time in months, and the guilt that you were forced to suffer when you willingly embraced the inhuman.

Jules was pushed down into the cannon. She tried to wriggle out, but one of the mutants said something to her – Cat supposed it was a threat to torture her son – and she let herself slide into it with a wretched, heartbreaking howl.

Mr Dowling patted George's head as he passed the distraught boy, then shoved Claudia aside – the crowd booed, but in a light-hearted way – and took hold of the control panel. He locked gazes with Cat and squealed shrilly.

'Bombs away!' Kinslow translated.

Then Mr Dowling pressed the button and Jules Bearman, Cat's sister, the person she had loved most in all the world since their parents passed on, was fired through the air and out into the stadium to be ripped to pieces by the ranks of living dead in the stands.

TWENTY

Cat buried her face in her hands and wept bitterly. To find her sister alive after all this time, and then to lose her so sickeningly ... She'd never thought the world could be this cruel. Then again, until today she'd never known that there was a world of mutants and telepathic, homicidal clowns.

Kinslow tapped her on the shoulder repeatedly until she moved her hands away and glanced up at him through her tears.

'Mr Dowling wants you,' the mutant said pleasantly.

Cat looked across at the clown. He was smiling and nodding at her while her nephew was being carried up to the cannon.

Cat wailed and covered her face with her hands again.

'Don't be like that,' Kinslow cooed. 'Maybe he wants to cut a deal. Maybe you can save the little boy if you hurry.'

'You really think so?' Cat moaned, peering at Kinslow through the cracks in her fingers, not daring to believe there might be any hope.

'There's only one way to find out,' Kinslow said with a twinkling grin.

Cat was certain that she was being toyed with, but regardless of that she got to her feet and staggered into the ring. If there was any possibility that she could save poor George, she had to take it before it slipped away. After all, there were no second chances in life.

'Aunty Cat!' George cried with shock when he spotted her.

She cringed, but forced herself to look up at the

shrieking boy and smile. 'It's OK, George. I'm going to sort this out.'

'Mummy?' George roared. 'Daddy?'

'They're fine,' she lied. 'They're waiting for you outside. But I'll see if I can get the clown to let you walk out to join them, so that you don't have to be fired through the air like they were.'

She didn't know whether or not George believed her. Before he could ask any more questions, he was pushed down into the cannon by the mutant who had carried him up to it.

Cat faced the smirking Mr Dowling and said, 'What do I have to do?'

The clown held out the cannon's control to her.

'You're out of your bloody mind!' Cat shouted. 'I'm not going to execute my own nephew!'

Mr Dowling cocked his head, his eyes darting wildly round his sockets, and he made a series of whining noises.

'He says you can swap places with the boy if you wish,' Kinslow said behind her.

Cat shuddered, but she had anticipated this and

resigned herself to it. 'OK,' she sighed. 'If that's what it takes.'

She started foward, to climb up and rescue her nephew, prepared to sacrifice herself for him. She had seen other people do this when attacked by zombies, give themselves up in an attempt to save a loved one. She'd always considered them the most foolish of fools, but it was different when it was one of your own.

As Cat took hold of the ladder, she paused and turned.

'How do I know that you'll let him go?' she asked.

Kinslow laughed. 'We never said we'd let him go.'

Cat's face fell. 'But you promised . . .'

'No, no, no, no, no,' Kinslow tutted. 'Mr Dowling only said you could swap places with the boy. He never said anything about what would happen to him after you were dead.'

'What *will* happen to him?' Cat asked.

Kinslow shrugged. 'I've no idea. Mr Dowling might let him go, or turn him into a mutant like me, or send him back up to be fired out of the cannon after you.'

'I need to know,' Cat groaned.

'You can't,' Kinslow said. 'We're not offering you a deal, just a chance to buy the boy some time. After that, his destiny lies in the lap of the gods. Well, in the lap of Mr Dowling.'

Cat stared at the mutant with horror and her hands fell by her sides.

'Please,' she whispered.

'Save your breath,' Kinslow sniffed. 'Are you swapping places or not?'

'I will if I can save him,' Cat wept. 'But if you're going to kill him anyway ...'

'We might not,' Kinslow reminded her.

'I need a guarantee,' she shouted.

'Mr Dowling isn't in the guaranteeing business,' Kinslow replied coolly. 'Now, are you climbing up there or not?'

Cat shook her head uncertainly. 'I need a minute to think about it. I ...'

Mr Dowling made a low, guttural noise.

'What did he say?' Cat asked.

Kinslow chuckled heartlessly. 'He said he would grant you a favour and do your thinking for you.'

And, with that, Mr Dowling pressed the button and George Bearman, Cat's eight-year-old nephew, was sent shooting to his doom, leaving his aunt to collapse to her knees in the centre of the ring and wail wretchedly while mourning all that she had lost.

TWENTY
-ONE

An uncontrollably sobbing Cat was led back to the throne and once again placed on Mr Dowling's lap. He cradled her this time and hummed to her as she wept, while Kinslow rounded up a small group of mutant violinists to play sad tunes.

The circus acts continued while Cat was crying. An undead knife-thrower threw knives at a nervous mutant, who ducked and shimmied out of the way of the blades until one caught him in the thigh and put him down — he hopped out of the ring to a chorus of catcalls. A zombie plate-spinner proved surprisingly nimble and managed to keep most of her plates aloft, even when three of them were topped with heads from some of the trapeze artists whose bodies had been smashed earlier. Two zombies parading around on stilts drew a warm round of applause, but a third member of the troupe kept falling over — the crowd booed until the stilts were set on fire and the flames engulfed the clumsy zombie.

The grieving Cat didn't even notice when an undead sword-swallower came forward and Mr Dowling plucked all of Cat's knives from her, to be used in the act. In her stunned state, she could only obsess about Jules, Paul and George, replaying the moments when they had been shot from the cannon over and over inside her head.

Finally there was a lull and silence fell over the crowd. The lack of noise eventually registered with Cat and she looked around in a daze, wondering if all of the mutants and babies had slipped out and left her.

No such luck. They were still here, but now they were leaning forward and staring mutely at her, as if waiting for her to do something.

'Here,' Kinslow grunted, handing her a handkerchief. 'Wipe your cheeks. You look a mess.'

'I don't care,' Cat whispered, letting the handkerchief drop.

Kinslow scowled, picked up the hankie, spat on it, then wiped Cat's cheeks clean. 'That's better,' he said. 'Though a touch of lipstick and mascara wouldn't go amiss. Do you have a handbag?'

He laughed at his little joke. Cat just stared at him numbly.

Mr Dowling whined and Kinslow stopped laughing. 'He says this isn't a time for laughter,' he muttered. 'Rather, it's time for the main performance. It's a serious act, deserving of our respect.'

'I don't care,' Cat said again, staring at the hole in the roof, wishing she had climbed up into the cannon and been fired off into oblivion.

'You should care,' Kinslow said with a smirk, 'because you're the star of this particular act.'

And with that he took her hand, helped her to her feet, then led her forward into the spotlights, where both her future and her past were waiting.

TWENTY
-TWO

Cat blinked with confusion as Kinslow positioned her in the centre of the ring. It seemed much bigger than it had earlier. Everything had been cleared away and it was just the two of them, Mr Dowling and all of the mutants and babies looking on from outside with fascination.

'You wanted to know why we chose you,' Kinslow said softly. 'Why, out of all the survivors in London, we selected you for special treatment. This is where you find out.'

Zombies advanced into the ring, several of them,

no handlers in sight. Catching the scent of Cat's brain, they set their sights on her and began to close in for the kill. Then Kinslow pressed a whistle between his lips and blew commandingly. The zombies drew to a halt and held their ground, eyeing Cat hungrily.

'We were at your school on Z day,' Kinslow said, stepping away from Cat to slowly circle the zombies. 'We'd been keeping tabs on one of your students.'

'Who?' Cat frowned, trying to think which of her useless pupils might be of interest to creatures such as these. 'Why?'

'We saw you sacrifice some of the children to the zombies in order to escape,' Kinslow went on, side-stepping her question. 'We admired your ruthless streak. We kept an eye on you after that, to see how you'd develop. We thought you might make a valuable addition to the team.'

'*Your* team?' Cat's nose wrinkled with disgust. 'Never.'

'Oh, I'm pretty sure you'd join us if the offer was put before you,' Kinslow snickered. 'Even given what we did to your sister and her family, I still think you'd do anything necessary to spare your own neck. And we might yet make that offer. Mr Dowling is weighing it up even as we speak.'

Cat's gaze flickered to the seated clown. He was looking all around the place and scratching an armpit. It was impossible to tell what he might be thinking.

'What would I have to do?' Cat asked warily.

'Tame the savage beasts,' Kinslow giggled, then blew his whistle again. At his command the zombies shuffled out of the ring and returned with steps and hoops which they set in place, reacting to Kinslow's orders. Claudia reappeared, adjusted some of the props, then set one of the hoops alight, before taking a little bow.

When the girl retreated, Kinslow blew his whistle shrilly and the zombies all climbed the steps, one per set, to balance on a single leg at the top. The mutants and babies applauded.

Kinslow blew again and a couple of the zombies did handstands. More applause. He then had the zombies descend to trot round the hoops and jump through one at a time, building up to the fiery hoop, which he kept until last.

A few of the zombies singed their heads or arms coming through the hoop of flames, but none suffered any serious injuries, and soon they were all standing in a line in front of Kinslow again, awaiting his next command.

'See?' Kinslow smiled. 'It's easy, isn't it?' He produced another whistle and tossed it to Cat. His face went flat and he said in a low voice, 'Your turn.'

TWENTY -THREE

Cat stared at the whistle, then looked up at the zombies, who hadn't moved.

'I can't control them,' she said.

'Then you're in trouble,' Kinslow laughed.

Cat gulped. 'I don't know how. You've got to help me, show me, give me advice, something.'

Kinslow shook his head. 'No help. Sink or swim. That's the way it is with us.'

Cat looked pleadingly at Mr Dowling. 'You can't do this to me,' she yelled. 'You went to all the trouble of tracking me, putting on this show, dragging my sister's family into it. You can't just let me be ripped to pieces now. What's the point of that?'

'Mr Dowling doesn't always need a point,' Kinslow said. 'But in this case he does have one. You might be able to figure out what it is if I tell you that the name of this act is *Cat Ward's Apt Finale*.'

Cat stared at Kinslow, completely at a loss. He waited for the penny to drop. When it didn't, he sighed and put the whistle between his lips, to blow one last time and set the zombies free of his influence.

Mr Dowling made a high wailing noise and stopped him.

Kinslow listened to his master, then nodded obediently. 'You're in luck,' he told Cat. 'Mr Dowling is granting you a lifeline. He's prepared to free you from your role in the act and offer you a place among his most trusted handservants.'

'What if I don't want it?' Cat asked.

'Then you'll die,' Kinslow said.

'Maybe I'd prefer to die,' Cat croaked.

Kinslow shook his head. 'You'd enjoy life as a

mutant. We're the same as you — hard, cold, merciless killers. In fact you're harder and colder than most of us. You're better suited to life as one of Mr Dowling's assistants than just about anyone else in the gang. We would have automatically recruited you ages ago if not for your association with somebody else we've been keeping an eye on.'

'What are you talking about?' Cat asked.

'Mr Dowling has a question for you,' Kinslow answered indirectly. 'Your response will determine what we do with you, whether we accept you as one of us or leave you to see out the act.'

'What question?' Cat cried, hating the mystery.

Kinslow waited a heartbeat, then said slyly, 'What did you think of your student, Becky Smith?'

Cat blinked. Of all the questions in the world, that was one of the last she had expected. 'Becky Smith?' she repeated.

'Yeah,' Kinslow said. 'You remember her?'

'Of course.'

'What was your opinion of her?'

Cat thought about answering truthfully, telling them

that the girl had been a horrid little beast, arrogant, rude, disruptive, a bully and a borderline racist. But the mutants seemed to approve of people with antisocial tendencies. If they were thinking of signing up Becky Smith, Cat wanted to do whatever she could to dissuade them. She could tolerate serving a master like Mr Dowling, and she was willing to work hand in hand with an army of mutant killers, but teaming up with a wretch like Becky Smith … a girl who had openly mocked her in class … that was a bridge too far.

'She was a weak, pitiful nothing,' Cat said dismissively. 'A mouthy, ignorant little scumbag who was clearly never going to amount to anything. I taught a lot of lousy kids over the years, but she was one of the most pathetic. I can't even say that I despised her, because she wasn't worthy of contempt.'

Kinslow hooted. The mutants in the audience gasped. The babies made an angry hissing noise and their eyes suddenly turned a deep red colour. On the throne, Mr Dowling sat bolt upright and glared at her, his eyes steady in their sockets for the first time since Cat had been introduced to him.

'Wait,' Cat cried, realising she had made a mistake. 'I didn't mean that. Becky was a wonderful girl, an exemplary student. She –'

'Too late,' Kinslow interrupted. 'Your first answer is the only one that we'll accept, and it was about as wrong as wrong could be.'

'But I don't understand,' Cat roared as Kinslow raised his whistle again. 'What was so special about Becky bloody Smith?'

'You'll find out,' Kinslow crowed. Then he smiled mockingly. 'Or, rather, you won't.'

Then, as he stepped backwards into the shadows, disappearing from sight, he stuck the whistle between his lips and blew, and the zombies in the ring were unleashed.

TWENTY
-FOUR

The undead shook their heads, bunched together, fixed their sights on Cat and advanced. She blew her whistle several times, as loudly as she could, but the zombies ignored her as she'd guessed they would.

Spitting out the whistle, Cat reached for a knife, only to find all of her scabbards bare. In a panic, she scrabbled for her gun but that was gone too. She glanced with horror at Mr Dowling on his throne and spotted him idly twirling the gun around. He must have smoothly removed it when he rid her of her knives, though she couldn't remember how exactly that had happened.

Despite her desperation, Cat backed up slowly, not wanting the zombies to break rank and race after her. She looked around for anything that she might be able to defend herself with, but the floor had been swept clean.

There was a gap in the barrier around the ring to Cat's left and that was what she edged towards. If she could get out of the enclosure, she would duck into the crowd. The mutants and babies might lose their composure if the pack of zombies came racing towards them. In the ensuing chaos, she might be able to sneak away and escape from the tent. Of course there were the tens of thousands of zombies outside to deal with, but she would cross that bridge if she came to it. One crisis at a time.

Cat kept expecting the zombies to attack. Those she'd encountered before had always reacted the same way in the presence of the living, hurling themselves at people, in a hurry to rip their skulls open and scoop out their brains. But these creeps held their formation and closed in slowly, steadily.

Cat was almost at the gap when a couple of figures stepped forward to block her way. They were girls in school uniforms. The uniforms were ripped, bloody and dusty, but Cat recognised the colours and the crest. They were from her old school.

Cat drew to a halt and stared at the pair of grim-faced zombies who had blocked her way. She'd spent a lot of her time since the fall of civilisation remembering these faces, so she identified the girls immediately.

They were two of the students she had thrown to the zombies in the laboratory at her school.

With a soft moan of understanding, Cat cast her gaze over the rest of the zombies in the ring. She hadn't focused on their faces before this, simply assuming them to be random members of the undead, as the other performers had been. But now that she studied them she realised they were all people she had knocked aside and left for the living dead when making good her own escape.

There was another of her students, one who had

almost made it to the exit, whom Cat had slammed into a wall and left behind, dazed and lost.

A man in a suit who'd taken shelter in an apartment close to her hidey-hole in a tower block, in the days before she'd decided to avoid such buildings. She'd woken to sniffing noises downstairs one night – she was a light sleeper, which had saved her on more than one occasion – and snuck into his room to tie him up and leave him behind as a distraction for the zombies while she climbed up on to the roof and waited there for morning.

A woman a few years older than Cat. They'd both been foraging one day and had been spotted by a young, fast zombie. As they fled side by side, Cat stuck out a leg and tripped up the woman. Her screams had chased Cat down the road, but not for long.

Cat sank to the floor in a broken heap, staring at the zombies as they crowded in above her, fangs glinting in the spotlights, fingers flexing. She recognised every face, each one of them a person who had paid with their life following a run-in with the ruthless ex-teacher.

If zombies ate the brains of all their victims, none of these people could have come back to haunt Cat Ward. But, as she'd noted before, the undead had some sort of inbuilt mechanism that programmed them to convert more people than they killed, and these had all been transformed rather than devoured.

'I'm sorry,' Cat whispered, but in truth she didn't mean it and, even if she had, it would have served no purpose. It was far too late for apologies.

Cat knew there was no way that she would be spared. These zombies were set to kill mode. They were going to smash open her skull, pull out every last sliver of her brain and tuck in. She wasn't sure if they had any idea that they would be eating the brain of the woman who had cost them their lives, but she wondered if on some subconscious level they would feel at least a little glow of satisfaction.

Then the fingerbones of the undead were upon her, digging into her head as she screamed her final scream, and the last thing she thought before she passed beyond the world of thinking was that, even if there were no second chances in life, the revenge that these zombies were enjoying was proof that sometimes, in death, there were.

"A CLEVER MIX OF HORROR, FANTASY AND REALISM... GRIPPING"
TELEGRAPH

ZOM-B BABY
DARREN SHAN
THE MASTER OF HORROR

ZOM-B GLADIATOR
DARREN SHAN
THE MASTER OF HORROR

ZOM-B MISSION
DARREN SHAN
THE MASTER OF HORROR

SCARY JUST GOT SERIOUS...

WWW.ZOM-B.CO.UK

SCAN FOR
MORE SHAN